DATE DU

44912

# TALL TINA

**Story by Muriel Stanek**
**Illustrated by Lucy Hawkinson**

**Albert Whitman & Company · Chicago**

*Books by Muriel Stanek*
NEW IN THE CITY
ONE, TWO, THREE FOR FUN
LEFT, RIGHT, LEFT, RIGHT!

STANDARD BOOK NUMBER 8075-7758-8
LIBRARY OF CONGRESS CARD NUMBER 79-126436
TEXT © 1970 BY MURIEL STANEK
ILLUSTRATIONS © 1970 BY ALBERT WHITMAN & COMPANY
PUBLISHED SIMULTANEOUSLY IN CANADA BY
GEORGE J. McLEOD, LIMITED, TORONTO
LITHOGRAPHED IN U.S.A.

*On Feeling Different from Others . . .*

Many children are sensitive about size or some other physical characteristic that makes them feel different from their friends. One child under such circumstances may react aggressively to criticism and teasing. Another may withdraw from the group and seek some kind of compensation. Happily, many of these problems, especially if associated with growth, are resolved with time and maturity. But this period can often be a painful one for the sensitive child.

In this story, Tina is not too self-conscious about being tall until she is teased by a new classmate. At first she reacts with anger and discomfort. Then she retreats from her friends, but daydreams of confronting the boy who taunted her. The problem is resolved as both Tina and the boy learn about the pain of being teased and begin to recognize that differences can have value. Tina's long legs, for example, make her a speedy runner and help her make her team in a relay race the winner.

This story will have special meaning for girls who are taller than other children of the same age. It also suggests insights in dealing with a boy like Jonathan who is aggressive but not particularly secure.

When children put themselves in the role of one or more characters in a book, they may, hopefully, gain a better understanding of their own feelings and those of others. Perhaps it will help them accept themselves as worthwhile persons.

—MURIEL STANEK

When Tina was little, everybody at home called her Tiny Tina. But as she grew taller and taller and went to school, it was only Grandma who still called her Tiny Tina.

"Tiny, please find my glasses," Grandma would say.

"Here they are, Grandma," Tina would call. "Right up here on the shelf."

That would make Grandma smile, and she'd say, "My Tiny Tina is getting tall, and that's fine. There are lots of tall people in our family."

It was true. Most of Tina's family were tall.

Aunt Mary took a good look at Tina one day and said, "Tina, you're going to be as tall as your mother. I'm sure of it."

Tina liked that. She was proud to look like her mother.

When Tina's father measured her and her big sister Beth, he said, "Well, what do you know! You two girls are the same size. Maybe I'll call you my twins."

Beth and Tina of course didn't look like real twins. But sometimes they were able to fool Mother just the same.

Once when they were outdoors, the girls traded coats.

"Beth," Mother called from the kitchen window. "Come here. I want you to go to the store."

But it wasn't Beth who turned around to answer Mother. It was Tina!

"You fooled me!" Mother said, and that made Tina and Beth laugh. Then they both went to the store for Mother.

Tina liked being tall when she and her mother went shopping for coats and dresses.

"We'll look for your new dress in the school girls' department," Mother said. "Dresses in the little children's section are too small for you now."

Tina agreed. "Those are little kid clothes," she said. "I like the big girls' dresses better."

Tina and Mother did their shopping. Then they had lunch in a restaurant.

"Remember when you had to sit on a little seat on a chair to make you tall enough to eat at the table?" Mother asked.

"And before that, I needed a high chair," Tina said. "I can't believe I was ever that little."

At school, Tina was the tallest girl in her room. Most of the time, this was fine with Tina.

Miss Green would say, "Tina, please get the paper from the top shelf in the cupboard."

"Not everyone can do that," Tina would say to herself.

Because she was tall, Tina had long legs and could run fast.

On the way to school, she would call to Robbie, "Bet you can't catch me!"

"You always win," Robbie would say. "That's because you have those long legs."

When the class had a spring play, Miss Green chose Tina to be a tree. Once or twice Tina wished she could be one of the little birds, pretending to fly around the stage.

But on the day of the play, Tina was happy and excited. She stood in the middle of the stage where everyone could see her. She wore a tall, leafy hat and stretched her arms out to make them look like branches.

There were other trees, but Tina was the tallest in the make-believe forest.

The music played, and Tina waved her branches gently above the others. It was fun.

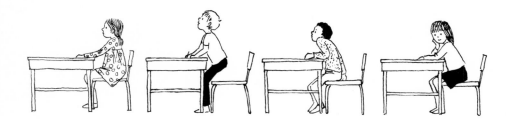

Sometimes, of course, Tina did wish she were shorter. She didn't like to sit in the last seat in her row.

One morning Tina tried to take a seat in the front of the room.

Miss Green saw her and said, "Tina, you're too tall for that seat. Billy can't see over your head."

Tina walked slowly back to her old seat at the back of the room.

At home, Tina was getting too tall to squeeze down into her favorite hiding place under the little round table.

"I see you!" Beth would call.

Even when Tina tried to curl up, the cloth never quite hid her.

Tina's favorite blanket was too short now. When she tried to cover herself with it, her feet stuck out.

Mother saw the trouble she was having. "Here's a big new blanket to keep you warm in bed," she said.

Tina pulled the new blanket over her. She twisted and turned and wiggled, but the new blanket still covered all of her.

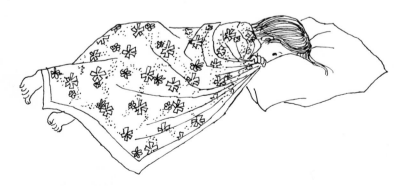

Because Tina was so tall, everyone expected her to act as grown up as Beth.

"You are too big to act silly," her father said when she giggled too much.

"You're too big to cry like a baby," Aunt Mary said when Tina tore her new dress.

Grandma was the only one who still treated Tina like a little girl.

"Tiny Tina," Grandma would say, "come and sit on my lap."

When Tina's throat was sore, she was glad to have someone to hold her. But when Grandma tried to rock, Tina's long legs dangled to the floor. Finally Tina slipped off Grandma's plump lap and put her head against Grandma's knee. Grandma stroked her hair.

A new boy named Jonathan moved into Tina's neighborhood. He was in her class at school. He was a short boy, but he seemed older than the other children.

On his first day at school, Jonathan saw Tina looking his way. He put his tongue out at her.

"Jonathan, we don't do that here," Miss Green said. "Stay after school and we'll talk about it."

"I don't care," Jonathan mumbled, and as the other children left, he put his foot out and tripped Billy.

A few days later, on the way home from school, Jonathan shouted, "Tina is a string bean—String Bean Tina!"

Some of the children laughed. Then somebody called, "Tall Tina! Look at Tall Tina!"

Tina ran home without looking back at any of the children who were teasing her.

Next morning there was a note on Tina's desk. When she unfolded it, she read, "Tina is a—" and there was a picture of a giraffe.

Tears filled Tina's eyes. "It's not my fault if I'm tall," she said to herself. She pulled her skirt down to hide her long legs and slid down into her seat.

Going home from school, Tina walked past the shopping center. She stopped to look at her tall reflection in the bakery window.

Suddenly she heard Jonathan calling, "Tall Tina! String Bean Tina!"

She ran toward home as fast as she could.

"I hate being tall," Tina told herself. "I've got to look shorter."

She tried walking with her knees bent and her shoulders stooped.

"How come you're walking like that?" her sister Beth asked.

"I have to look shorter," Tina answered.

"Who cares if you're tall? Mother and Aunt Mary are tall. They don't care," Beth said.

But Tina did care. She couldn't help it.

Tina sat in Grandma's
rocker. She thought about
what she'd like to say to
that Jonathan if he called
her names again.

"Mean,

      *mean,*

           MEAN!
You're mean, Jonathan!"
she whispered to herself.
"I'll tell him that if he
bothers me."

The next morning, Tina came to school early.

There was Jonathan on the playground. Tina hoped he wouldn't see her. She did not feel like fighting with him after all.

She squeezed behind the half-open school door and watched Jonathan through the crack.

Jonathan was teasing Billy. He called, "You're nothing but a little shrimp, that's all!"

"I'm just about as big as you are," Billy said.

Tina knew how Billy felt. She wanted to run out and help him. But the bell rang, and it was time for school to begin.

Now nothing seemed as much fun to Tina as it had. She began to think *everyone* was laughing at her because she was tall. At recess, she stayed indoors and helped clean the cupboard.

One afternoon when Tina was walking home, she turned around and saw Jonathan behind her. She ran as fast as she could toward a big fence. She hid behind it and peeked out from between the boards.

As Jonathan came closer, she saw he was not running after her at all. Two older boys were chasing him!

All at once Jonathan tripped, fell, and bumped his nose so hard it bled. There was a big red bump on his forehead.

While Tina watched, the big boys ran up and laughed at Jonathan. He had his hand to his nose and tears ran down his cheeks.

"Crybaby!" the boys yelled before they ran off.

Tina stayed behind the fence until the big boys had gone. She was all set to say, "Ha, ha, ha, Jonathan, serves you right! Now you know how it feels to have someone make fun of you."

But as Tina came over to Jonathan she didn't yell at him after all. She was surprised—she felt sorry for Jonathan!

She handed him her handkerchief, and he wiped his nose and slowly got up.

Tina and Jonathan walked down the street together without saying a word.

At Jonathan's house, they stood for a moment. Jonathan's nose had stopped bleeding, and the bump on his head didn't look too bad.

"Want to see my new kitten, Tina?" Jonathan asked.

Tina wondered if she had really heard Jonathan. For the first time he had used her right name and wasn't making fun of her.

"Maybe he isn't so bad after all," she thought. Still, she wasn't sure she wanted to be friendly so fast.

"My mother is waiting for me," she answered. "I'll stop and see your kitten some other time."

As she walked on toward home nobody called "Tall Tina!" or "String Bean!" That felt good.

Next morning, Tina looked at her desk to see if there were any mean notes from Jonathan. There weren't any.

When she went outside, she listened to hear if someone called teasing names. No one did.

A week went by. Not once did Tina hear anyone say anything about her size. She began to stand up straight and tall again.

Jonathan seemed to forget about Tina. But one day he asked her, "Want to use my new pen? It writes different colors."

Tina wasn't quite sure what to do. She thought, "Maybe he thinks I'll tell the other kids I saw him crying. But then, maybe he does want to be nice."

Looking up at Jonathan, she said, "I'll try it." And she drew a little stick man with a red hat and a blue coat. "It's a great pen," she said.

A warm spring day came, and the children were on the playground.

Mr. Scott, the gym teacher, called, "We're going to have relay races. Jonathan will be the captain of one team. Bill will be the captain of the other team. Captains, choose your teams!"

Billy chose Mark for his team. Then it was Jonathan's turn to choose.

"I take you!" he said, pointing to Tina.

"Why should I be on his team?" Tina asked herself, but she walked slowly toward Jonathan.

The teams lined up. The shortest runners were first and the tallest last. Mark was the last one on Billy's team. Tina was the last on Jonathan's team.

"Ready, set, GO!" called Mr. Scott.

Off Billy and Jonathan raced to the fence and then back to the next runners in line. The teams were so evenly matched it was hard to tell which would win.

Waiting to run, Tina and Mark jumped up and down. Tina felt she had to win. Mark felt *he* had to win.

It was a close race right to the very end.

"Run, Tina, run!" yelled Jonathan. Tina ran as hard as she could—she had to beat Mark.

Tina's long legs carried her over the finish line just ahead of Mark. She had done it! She had won for her team!

Everybody cheered. Jonathan shouted "We won!" the loudest of all and gave Tina a big smile.

That night, when Tina looked in the mirror at home, she stood straight and tall. She didn't stoop or slump. Being tall was a pretty good thing. She felt like herself again, glad to be in a tall family.